STILL WITH YOUR MEMORIES

A LETTER TO UNKNOWN YOU

JEEVITA GOWD

Made with ♥ on the Notion Press Platform
www.notionpress.com

I WANT TO DEDICATE THIS BOOK TO MYSELF .

FOR ENDURING ALL THE PAIN ALL ALONE .

Contents

Contents

Preface

THIS BOOK IS ALL ABOUT
THE LOVE OFTWO PERSONS
WHO NEVER MEET.
WHEN THEY STARTED LOVING
EACH OTHER WITHOUT
KNOWING EACH OTHER.
WHERE GIRL STILL WRITE THE
LETTER TO EXPRESS THE THOUGHTS
THAT SHE NEVER FORGET HIM

Acknowledgements

I WOULD LIKE TO SAY THANKS MY LATE MOTHER
AND MY LORD SAI BABA
AND THANKS FOR MYSELF FOR NOT GIVING UP
ON MYSELF WHEN WHOLE WORLD LEFT MY HAND

.

THIS BOOK IS PENNED AND EDITED BY ME
WITH MY OWN IMAGINATION.

Prologue

THIS BOOK CONSISTS OF BUNCH
OF LETTERS OF EMOTIONS.
WHICH EXPRESS THE FEELING OF THE LOVE .
THE LOVE WHICH HOLDS THE SPECIAL
POWER OF THIS BOTH UNSEEN PEOPLE .
THE LETTERS OF THE GIRL WHICH
EXPRESS THE TRUE EMOTIONS OF
WAITING FOR SOMEONE .
WHOM THERE IS NO ACTUAL EXISTENCE
BUT THE RELATION WHICH SHE BELIEVES .
HE EXISTS IN HER LIFE IN EVERY PHRASE .
WITHOUT HIS PHYSICAL PRESENCE.
TO WALK ON THE THRONE TO BLEED
HEART BY LOVING SOMEONE .
WHERE HEART AND SCIENCE
DOESN'T HAVE AN ANSWER .
THE HARDEST LOVE TO FEEL
THERE PRESENCE WITHOUT
KNOWING THERE EXISTENCE.
A FEELING OF CONECTIVITY BY PLAYING
WITH THE FIRE OF EMOTIONS

Author Bio

MEET THE AUTHOR MISS JEEVITA GOWD
SHE IS AN AUTHOR BY PASSION AND MODEL.
SHE COMPLETED HER GRADUATION.
HER HONOURS –
SHE WAS THE CO –AUTHOR OF 5 BOOKS
AND AUTHOR OF THE BOOKS
1-THE WAY TO SUCCESS BY ACCEPTING PAIN AND REALITY
2- LOVE STORY OF ALICE AND DANID.
3-CURSED ISLAND .
4-BOOK OF QUOTES
5-FADED DREAM OF PAST LIFE.
6-SUCCESS MINDSETS
7- TWIN FLAME –WHO ARE YOU?
AND IN WRITING FIELD SHE ACHIEVED
MOST PRESTIGIOUS AWARD GLORY AWARD
OF INDIA AS AN AUTHOR.
SHE IS FAMOUS HER QUOTES
SHE WAS FEATURED MANY MAGAZINES
LIKE TIMES OF SRINAGAR, TIMES OF AMERICA
TIMES OF UP
TIMES OF BOMBAY
HER HONOURS AS A MODEL
MISS BHARAT OF CHATTISGARH WINNER
MISS REPUBLIC OF INDIA SECOND RUNNER
AND SHE ALSO WALKED IN INTERNATIONAL RAMP.

Author Pick

AUTHOR -JEEVITA GOWD

1

ARE YOU THERE

ARE YOU THERE

CAN TIME STOPS AND LET ME
SEE YOU AGAIN AND AGAIN WITH
THE BLURRY EYES FILLED WITH THE
TEARS TO SEE YOU ONE LAST TIME .
CAN WE CHANGE THE TIME ?
CAN WE HOLD ON FOREVER ?
ARE YOU THERE ?
PLEASE HAVE A WARM NIGHT WITH BY
WINNING THE RACE OF DARKNESS .
THERE IS A NEW RAY EVERY TIME I SEE YOU .
WHEN THERE IS NOTHING GOING ON RIGHT .
YOU CAME LIKE A LIGHT TO ADD A NEW RAY
OF HOPE IN THE LIFE .
THE ANGELS DO EXISTS WHEN I SEE YOU SMILE .

2

YOU'RE MY THAT LOVE

YOU'RE MY THAT LOVE
LOVING YOU .
YOU'RE MY THAT LOVE WHICH DEATH
COULD NOT SEPRATE .
YOU'RE MY THAT LOVE WHICH SHINES BEAUTIFUL
LIKE THE MOON IN THE DARKNESS BUT THE LOVE
WHICH
COULDNOT REACH .
THE SHINE IN YOU BRIGHT SO MUCH WHICH
CANT BE SEEN WITH THE NAKED EYE.
YOUR THAT LOVE OF MINE WHICH I NEVER KNEW
BUT
WITHOUT THAT LOVE WHERE EXISTENSE
ITSELF HURTS.
FOR THAT BEAUTIFUL EYES CAN GO
AGAINST WHOLE WORLD.
YOU'RE MY THAT LOVE WHICH IS SO FAR BUT
NEAR WHERE MY HEARTS STARTS BEATING .
YOUR THAT LOVE OF MINE WHICH STARTS

WITH THE SACRIFICE .
WHERE LETTING GO OF YOU STARTS WITH
YOUR HAPPINESS .
THAT LOVE WHICH TIME DOESNOT HAVE
THE POWER TO ERASE .
THAT LOVE IF NOT YOU EVERYTHING WOULD
BE MISSING IN THE LIFE .
YOUR THAT DEPTH OF LOVE WHICH PEOPLE
ONLY IMAGINED .
THE TRUE DEPTH WHERE LOVE BEGINS
WITHOUT KNOWING EACH OTHER .
THE BLURED VISIONS OF YOURS COULDNOT BE
ERASED
BY THE TIME THE SOUL NEVER STOPS SEARCHING
FOR
YOUR EXISTENCE .
THE SCARS CANT BE HEALED WITHOUT YOU .

3

UNSAID WORD OF YOUR HEART

UNSAID WORD OF YOUR HEART

I UNDERSTAND HOW STRONG YOUR.
HOW STRONG YOU NEED TO BE .
EVERYONE SAW YOUR SMILE AND
FORGOT TO ASK YOUR SCARS .
CAN YOU NOT HURT YOUSELF ?
THE UNFORGETTABLE PAIN OF YOURS ARE
STILL UNDER THE BLANKETS .
DO YOU EVEN KNOW WHY
YOUR HEART IS ACHING?
WHY DO YOU STILL FEEL
THE PAIN .
YOU HAVE SEEN PEOPLE CHANGING
WHEN YOU NEED THEM THE MOST .
EVERY ONE WHO WAS CLOSE TO YOUR HEART
SOME OF THEM STABBED BACK WITH THE TRUST .
ITS HARD FOR YOU TO BELIEVE .
YOUR THAT PERSON WHO SAYS THAT YOU NEVER
CARE BUT IF YOU CARE YOU CAN NEVER

REPLACE THAT PERSON .
THEY BECOME YOUR WORLD YOU STILL AFRAID
OF EMOTIONS BECAUSE YOU NEVER FEEL
CONNECTED AND FEEL COMFORTABLE WITH
ANYONE EASILY .
FINDING YOURSELF ALL ALONE EVEN WHEN
WHOLE WORLD IS WITH YOU .
YOU HAVE EVERYTHING YOU NEED BUT STILL
WHAT
ARE YOU SEARCHING FOR ?
NOTHING HAS THE POWER TO MAKE YOU HAPPY .
YOU WANTED TO BE LOVED .
YOU WANT THAT CONNECTIVITY IN THE PEOPLE
YOU FEEL COMFORT WITH .
YOU WANT TO BE LOVED UNCONDITIONAL
EVEN IF YOU SHOW YOUR ALL SCARS .
THE PERSON WHO DOESN'T CARE
IF YOUR RICH OR
YOUR POOR WHO DOESN'T WANT
ANYTHING FROM YOU.
I WAIT FOR THAT DAY WHEN YOUR SMILE IS REAL.

4

SCARS ON YOUR SOUL

SCARS ON YOUR SOUL

YOU THAT LOVE OF MINE FOR THOSE
BEAUTIFUL SOUL.
EVERY MOMENT LOYALITY EXISTS WHERE
I HAVE EVERYTHING BUT THIS EYES SEARCH
FOR YOUR EXISTENCE IN MY EVERY STEP OF MY
LIFE .
MY HEART SAID WITH A SILENT VOICE YOUR STILL
THAT SMALL KID WHO CANT COME OUT OF
YOUR PAST .
YOUR HURT ,FEAR AND INSECURITY OF PAST
YOU STILL NEED A HAND TO SAY YOU.
THAT EVERYTHING
WILL BE ALRIGHT .
MY HEART ACHED WHEN I SAW YOU
SMILE WITH INVISIBLE WOUNDS .
WHEN YOUR CRYING WITH THE
SILENT TEARS .
THIS HANDS CANT WIPE THE SILENT

TEARS OF MINE SAYS
I AM WITH YOU THAT
YOUR NOT ALONE
I CRIED THAT I COULDNOT CHANGE
THE DESTINY .
I FEEL REGRET FOR NOT HEALING THAT
SMALL KID WHO IS STILL STUCKED IN PAST .
I REGRET ABOUT THE PEOPLE .
WHERE YOU WAS AN OPEN BOOK .
BUT EVERYONE PRAISED
ABOUT YOUR BEAUTY ,
TALENT BUT FORGOT TO SEE
INSIDE YOUR HEART .
YOUR SO STRONG .
I UNDERSTAND THE PAIN WHEN YOU CRIED IN
NIGHTS HOLDING YOUR MOUTH SO NO ONE
CAN LISTEN THE HEART ACHE OF YOURS .
YOU CRIED AND ACTED LIKE
NOTHING HAPPENED .
ACTED LIKE NOTHING CAN HURT YOU .
I AM PROUD OF YOU FOR BEING A PERSON
WHO IS BROKEN BUT BEAUTIFUL .
THE ANGER IN YOU HIDES
A LOT OF LOVE .
YOU HAVE A BEAUTIFUL HEART .
NO SITUATION HAS THE POWER
TO BREAK YOU .
YOU ARE ONLY WEAKNESS
IS YOUR EMOTIONS .
WHICH YOU ALWAYS HIDE .
BUT YOU WANT THE PERSON
WHO TRULY CARES
FOR YOU WHO CAN UNDERSTAND YOUR EVERY

UNSAID WORD.
JUST BY SEEING YOUR EYES CAN FEEL EVERY PAIN
YOU HAVE BEEN HIDING FROM THE AGES .
YOUR FEELINGS CANT BE HIDED
ANYMORE .
BECAUSE THE PERSON WHO TRULY CARES
WILL UNDERSTAND YOUR EVERY PAIN
WITHOUT BEING EXPRESSED BY YOU .
BECAUSE TRUE CARE STARTS WITH
HEART NOT LOGICAL.

5

CAN YOU PLEASE FIND ME ?

CAN YOU PLEASE FIND ME ?

CAN YOU PLEASE FIND ME
COULD YOU LISTEN MY VOICE?
CAN YOU HEAR ME ?
SILENT TEARS ARE TAKING OVER ME .
CAN YOU PLEASE FIND THE BROKEN PIECES
OF MY HEART WHICH IS SHATTERED?
CAN YOU PLEASE FIND THE ME
WHICH HAS BEEN LOST IN
THIS CUNNING WORLD.
CAN YOU GIVE ME THE SMILE
WHICH I HAVE LOST BEFORE THE AGES ?
CAN YOU ERASE ALL THE
SCARS ON MY SOUL ?
CAN YOU NOT LEAVE ME EVEN
WHEN WHOLE WORLD IS AGAINST ME?
CAN YOU PROVE TIME THAT
WE ARE NOT WEAK ?
CAN WE FIND EACH OTHER NO MATTER

WHAT TURN LIFE TAKES ?
CAN YOU WAIT FOR ME ?
CAN YOU PLEASE FIND ME ?
CAN YOU PLEASE MAKE THE TIME
WHICH COULDNOT ERASE OUR FOOT STEPS?
CAN WE CREATE A SEPRATE STORY
WHERE THERE IS NO END ?
CAN YOU PLEASE FIND ME ?
EVEN IF I AM WEARNING A
MASK OF HAPPINESS ?
CAN YOU FIND THE REAL ME
WHO IS STILL HIDING IN THE
OCEAN OF EMOTIONS ?
CAN YOU BE ABLE TO UNDERSTAND
THE DEPTH OF MY PAIN
EVEN IF I AM SIELNT .
WHICH IS STABBING ME WITH
THE INVISIBLE WOUNDS .

PAIN

CAN YOU ERASE THE REASON
FORYOUR EXISTENCE
THE THINGS WHICH HAS THE POWER
TO INFLUENCE YOU .
YOUR WEAKNESS .
YOUR EMOTIONS .
THE THINGS WHICH YOU COULDNOT
CONTROL OVER .
THE THINGS WHICH TIME DOESN'T HAVE THE
POWER TO ERASE THE MEMORIES .
YOUR KIND HEART WHICH S
BEATING NOW FOR THE HELP.
THE VOICE OF YOUR HEART
WHICH IS LEFT UNSAID .
THE PAIN OF YOUR CANT BE ERASED
WITH JUST SIMPLE TEARS .
THE PRESENT EMOTIONS OF LOOSING
YOUSELF IN THE WAVE OF PAIN .
BELONGING TO THE WORLD OF DARK .
WHERE EMOTIONS WERE TAKING OVER YOU .

HOW MUCH YOU WANT TO RUN AWAY FROM IT ?]

7

ITS NOT LOVE WHICH HURT

ITS NOT LOVE WHICH HURT

ITS NOT LOVE WHICH HURT .
IT'S THE PEOPLE WHO MADE
YOU HATE ON THE LOVE .
ITS NOT YOUR FAULT THAT YOU
BECOME COLD HEARTED .
WHEN YOU WAS SO KIND AND CRAVED
FOR THE TRUE EMOTIONS.
ITS PEOPLE RIGHT WHO MADE YOU LIKE THAT ?
ITS PEOPLE RIGHT WHO STABBED YOU
WITH THE KNIFE OF WORDS
CALLED TRUST .
ITS NOT YOU WHO WANTS TO BE ALONE .
ITS YOUR HEART WHICH SAID THAT IT DOESN'T
WANT TO GET BROKE AGAIN WITH
THE WORDS CALLED CHEAT .
ITS NOT YOUR MISTAKE TO BE BROKEN .
ITS NOT YOUR HEART WHICH STOPPED BEATING .
ITS NEED A HAND WHICH CAN HEAL THEM .

STILL WITH YOUR MEMORIES

CAN YOU BE OK UNTIL THEN.

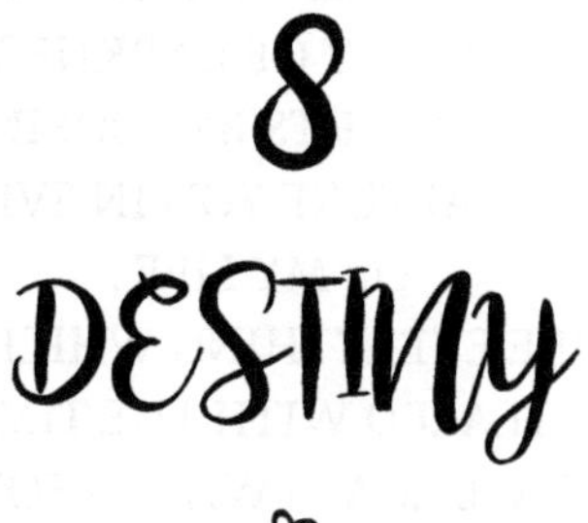

DESTINY

SOMEDAYS ITS REALLY HARD TO WOKE
UP BY MYSELF.
THE LOVE WILL NEVER BE GONE
I WANT TO BUILD THE DYANASTY
OF LOVE .
I WOULD GIVE YOU EVERY PIECE
OF MY HEART .
SO WHEN I FALL I COULD
GET BY HOLDING
YOUR HAND .
I WILL SMILE EVERYTIME EVEN AFTER
FALLING BECAUSE
I WILL BUILD THE DYNASTY OF LOVE .
I WILL NOT FALL .
I WOULD CHANGE CURSE ON MY SOUL TO
BRIGHTNESS IN MY LIFE .
SOMEDAY I COULD HOLD YOU WITHOUT
EVEN LETTING YOU GO .
THE DAY I WOULD HAVE EVERYTHING
WHICH I LOST .

I FIND MYSELF AGAIN .
I WONT FALL AGAIN IN THE
MYSTERY OF DARKNESS
OF MY THOUGHTS BY LOOSING YOU .
I WOULD CAPTURE YOU IN EVERY PAGE
OF MY LIFE .
I CAPTURE EVERYTHING WHICH CANT BE
STEALED WITH THE TIME .
I WONT FALL AGAIN WHEN I FOUND YOU .

9

THE UNFADED MEMORIES

THE UNFADED MEMORIES

THE RAYS OF YOUR MEMORIES .
LIVING WITH MY MEMORIES
I WILL COME OUT OF THE DILLEMMA .
I WILL SEARCH YOU NO MATTER
WHERE YOU EXIST IN THE MAZE OF WORLD .
THE FLAME OF BRIGHTNESS
YOU HELD WILL BE FOREVER .
FOR THE LIFE NO ONE IS HERE .
WHO CAN SAVE THE EXHAUSTED
SOUL OF MINE.
ITS NOT EASY TO BE ALONE .
IN EVERY SEASON I WISH
I COULD FIND YOU .
I CLOSE MY EYES WITH
THE BURDENED HEART
WHICH IS HARD TO
HANDLE BY MYSELF .
MY HEART WILL BE BROKEN EVERY

TIME I SEE MYSELF BREAKING AGAIN .
MY HEART SAYS ITS NOT
PERFECT TO BE ALONE .
IT REMINDS YOUR VISION .
IT WANTS TO GET DRUNKEN BY
THE THOUGHTS OF LOVE AND
WANTS TO FORGET IT
WHEN MORNING COMES .
YOU WERE IN MY ARMS WHEN
I WAS LYING MYSELF THAT I AM FINE .
WHEN I OPENED MY EYES
ITS JUST YOU AND
YOUR MEMORIES .
THE GIRL OF YOUR DREAM
THE SUNLIGHT OF YOUR DREAMS .
I AM HOLDING A BOQUE
OF HAPPINESS FOR YOU .
HOLDING A MAGIC IN MY HANDS
TO HEAL YOUR EXAUSTED SOUL.
WAITING TO SEE THE BEST
VERSION OF YOUR SELF .
THE PERSON WHO CAN HOLD YOUR
HAND AND TAKES YOU
THE WORLD OF HAPPINESS .
AND SAY YOU NOTHING IS GONNA
BE WRONG WHEN EVERYTHING
IS THE TERRIFIC .
HOLDING A MAGICAL BALLON TO SAY
YOU .
I WILL THEIF EVERY STRESSFULL
SITUATION OF YOURS.
WHEN YOU FEEL COLD HOLDING
THE RAYS OF WARMTH .

HOLDING A ANNIVESARY OF
EVERY HAPPY MOMENTS WE HAD
IN OUR DREAMS WHICH WERE NEVER REAL.
TO BE THE RAY IN YOUR LIFE IN THE DARKNESS.

10
HEARTBREAK

HEART BREAK

DO YOU EVEN THINK OF ME ?
DO YOU EVEN KNOW THE
DARKNESS IN MY LIFE .
DO YOU EVEN KNOW HOW MUCH
I NEEDED YOU IN THE LIFE .
DO YOU EVEN KNOW HOW MUCH I BEGGED
THE DESTINY TO SHOW YOU ONCE .
DO YOU EVEN KNOW HOW MANY
SILENT NIGHTS I SPENT BY MYSELF .
BY SAYING I WILL BE OK WHEN I AM NOT ?
CAN YOU EVEN IMAGINE ME.
WHEN THERE IS NO LIGHT IN MY LIFE .
WHERE THERE IS NO LOVE IN MY LIFE .
WHERE I STARTED DOUBTING ON
MY EXISTENCE .
PASSING OF THE SEASON WINTER
WAITED FOR THE
ANOTHER SEASON JUST BY WAITING
ON THE BALCONY SILENTLY .
HOLDING A SMILE TOWARDS THE MOON .

SHARING THE DEEPEST SECRETS OF MINE .
WHERE I HOLDED THE HEART
WHICH BLEEDS EVERY MINUTE .
I WAS WEAK .
I WAS AFRAID .
I WAS LOST IN THE DARKNESS .
WAS WITH THE MOON BY
HOLDING HOPES UP .
BUT NO ONE TO CATCH THE FALLEN ME .

11

I REGRET

I REGRET
NO ONE TO SAVE YOU
SOMETIMES THE PAIN IN YOU
ACHED MY HEART TO DEATH .
THE REGRET FOR NOT BEEN ABLE
TO HOLD YOU WHEN YOU FALL .
WHEN YOU DIED EMOTIONALLY
EVERY MOMENT IN LIFE .
I COULDNOT BE ABLE
TO HOLD YOU .
I COULD MAKE YOU FEEL SAFE .
I COULDNOT BE ABLE TO HOLD
THE EXAUSTED YOU .
I COULDNOT BE ABLE
TO SEARCH YOU .
I WISH I COULD BE ABLE
TO LOVE YOU .
I WISH I CAN WRITE YOUR
NAME ON MY VEINS .
I WISH I COULD HOLD BACK
THE BLURRED MEMORIES OF YOURS.

THE LOVE WHICH WAS NEVER REAL
BY SEARCHING YOU WITHOUT
KNOWING YOUR SMELL.
THE JOURNEY I STARTED HOLDING
MY WORLD WITH THE ONLY MEMORIES.

12

MY WORLD WITH THE ONLY MEMORIES.

MY WORLD WITH THE ONLY MEMORIES

CAN WE HAVE A SINGLE DAY
CAN WE JUST HAVE SINGLE DAY
WHERE I COULD CALL YOU MINE .
WHERE I CAN SAY YOU THAT
I EXIST FOR YOU .
CAN WE JUST HOLD HANDS AND SPEND
THE TIME LIKE IT WAS THE LAST DAY .
LOVING YOU WAS NEVER
AN EASY TASK .
THE PAIN OF SEPRATION WILL
BE TAKEN OVER ME .
THE THINGS CALLED FATE WOULD BE
GONE FOREVER IN MY LIFE.
THAT ONE DAY I WOULD BE LIVING
LIKE THE REAL ME .

HAVING NO CONCERN
ABOUT TOMMOROW .
WHERE I WILL BE CAPTURING THE
MEMORIES IN THE PAGES OF MY LIFE .

13

CAN I CALL YOU MY FATE OR DESTINY ?

<u>CAN I CALL YOU MY FATE OR DESTINY ?</u>

CAN I CALL YOU MY DESTINY OR FATE ?
LIVING WITHOUT EACH OTHER BUT
LIVING FOR EACH OTHER .
I HOLDED YOUR HANDS WITHOUT
KNOWING YOU .
YOU CANT ESCAPE FROM THIS FATE .
THE FATE WHICH MAKES
US HATE ON
LOVE SO ONE DAY WE COULD
HEAL EACH OTHER .
THE THINGS CALLED AFFECTION IN
OUR LIFE HAS BEEN MISSED OUT .
CAN WE FILL THE GAP OF THE LOVE BY
ACCEPTING THE FLAWS OF EACH OTHER .
THE DEPTH OF PAIN COULDNOT

BE HEALED WITH THE TIME .
I FOUNDED A HAPPINESS
IN THE RAYS OF YOUR VOICE .
NO MATTER WHERE YOU RUN AWAY
WE WILL FIND EACH OTHER BECAUSE
WE CANT GO AGAIN
THE WRITTEN DESTINY OF EACH OTHER.

14

THE CRUEL DEATH OF SOUL

THE CRUEL DEATH OF SOUL

THE CRUEL DEATH OF MY SOUL
CAN YOU NOT KILL ME WITH
THIS EMOTIONAL BURDEN
OVER MY HEART .
CANT YOU GO EASY ON ME ?
FOR LOVING YOU .
CAN YOU CARE A LITTLE .
I WONT BE ABLE TO TAKLE
THE PAIN OVER MY HEART ?
WOULD I BE ABLE TO SURVIVE AGAIN
WITHOUT YOUR EXISTENCE IN MY LIFE.
WILL I BE GLAD TO SEE YOU IN PAIN
WHEN YOU WOKE UP FROM OUR
DREAMS OF MEMORIES .
CAN I STILL CALL THIS WORLD
AS BEFORE IT USED TO BE .
THERE IS NO ONE WHO CAN HOLD ME
AND SAY I WILL BE FINE ONE DAY .

ARE YOU REALLY THAT COLD ?
THAT YOU KILLED MY INNOCENT SOUL .

15

YOUR LOVE WAS NEVER THE LOVE

YOUR LOVE WAS NEVER THE LOVE

YOUR LOVE WAS NEVER THE LOVE.
YES I BELIEVED IN YOU .
I BELIEVED THAT YOU NEVER
LEAVE THE HAND OF MINE .
I WAS LEAVING BUT YOU
NEVER STOPPED .
I WASN'T HEALING .
YOUR LOVE BECAME A
CURSE TO MY SOUL .
WHERE YOU BECAME
THE WEAKNESS WHICH I CANT RESISTS .
THE BELIEF I HAD ON YOU BROKEN
WITH THE TIME .
LOVE TURNED TO HATE
WITH A PROMISE TO
NEVER SEE YOU AGAIN .
A PROMISE TO NOT FALL FOR
THE TRAP OF ILLUSIONS .

WHICH GONNA EXAUSHT ME
OVER THE TIME PERIOD.
BECAUSE YOU NEVER GONNA
UNDERSTAND THE DEPTH
OF MY EMOTIONS .
YOU LEFT THE LETTER UNREAD .

16

CAN WE?

<u>CAN WE?</u>

THE STORM IN MY HEART WAS
KILLING ME INSIDE .
THE PAIN TOOK OVER ME
YOUR VOICE HOLDED A DEPTH
WHICH MADE MY HEART BEAT AGAIN .
CAN WE STAY UNTIL I FORGET TO
BREATH AND DISSOLVE IN THE AIR .
SOMETIMES I FEEL
I WAS DESTROYED INTO FALLEN PIECES
THEN SUDDENLY A REASON CAME UP
SHOWED A LIGHT JUST TO BE ALIVE
IN THIS CRUEL WORLD .
CAN WE JUST STAY UNTIL
MY LAST GOODBYE .

17

you

YOU

A POWER TO HOLD YOU .
EVEN WHEN YOU ARE ABOUT TO FALL.
THE TEARS WHICH FELT FROM
YOUR EYES .
A LIFE LONG REVENGE WITH THE
PEOPLE WHO MADE YOU CRY .
A PROMISE TO YOUR HANDS
WHICH NEVER BE ALONE AGAIN.
EVEN DEATH DOESN'T HOLD THE POWER
TO SEPRATE YOUR SOUL AWAY FROM.
WHEN YOU WERE LIKE A KID HOLDING
YOUR FEARS BUT NO EYES CAUGHT
ATTENTION OF THE PAIN YOU WERE
HIDING OF FROM THE WORLD .
YOU ADDED A LIFE TO MY
EXHAUSTED SOUL .
THE SOUL WHICH MAY MEET
THE DEATH AND BE ALIVE AGAIN JUST
TO HOLD YOU IN MY ARMS

18

CAN YOU?

<u>CAN YOU?</u>

CAN YOU NOT BREAK
THE TRUST .
WHICH I HAVE GAVE YOU .
THE EMOTIONS WHICH MADE
ME BURDENED WITH THE TIME .
TIME STARTED SHOWING
THE REALITY OF DUAL FACES .
SHOWN THE HIDDEN MASK .
WHICH FELT REAL BY HEART .
WAS A CHILD TO
BELIEVE YOU WAS REAL.
MY ANXIETY WAS GIVEN
A NAME OF MADNESS .
LOVE WOULD BREAK
THE CHAIN OF BURDEN .
WE COULD HOLD THE THINGS
BETTER WITH A PHASE TO
HOLD OURSELVES .

19

TRUST

<u>TRUST</u>

NO BRO IS NOT AVAILABLE .
THE LIVING CREATURES PLAYED.
THE WELL KNOWN KIND ROLE
WITH HOLDING A LIE CALLED TRUST .
TRUST A SIMPLE FIVE LETTER WORDS
COULD LET PEOPLE NEVER SAY A
LAST GOODBYE WHEN ITS BROKEN .
THE POWER TO MAKE KIND HEARTED
TO YOUR POWERFUL ENEMY
WHEN ITS BROKEN WITH THE LIE
OF CARE AND DUAL FACES .
A STARTED JOURNEY HOLDED FOR A
LONG TERM BREAK WHEN IT
UNDERSTOOD THE WORDS FILLED
WITH CUNNINGNESS OF THE PEOPLE.
THE LIE WHICH CANNOT BE CHANGED
THE LEFT PERSON WOULD NEVER BE BACK .
WHEN THIS WORDS TOUCHED THE VOICE OF SOUL.

20

YES?

YES?

THERE WOULD BE
NO WORDS.
THE WORDS WHICH WILL
BE LEFT UNSAID.
THE CONNECTION WONT BE
BOUNDED AGAIN .
THE HANDS WONT HOLD YOU
WHEN YOU WERE COLD .
LOVE TO STRANGER A LONG DISTANCE
CROSSED WITH THE WEIGHT OF
A SINGLE WORD .
THE WORDS WHICH MADE
BLEED OF EMOTIONS .
THE SCARS WONT BE FILLED AGAIN
WITH THE WORDS
CALLED TRUST.
EGO REPLIED HEART LEFT
THE PLACE EMPTY .
BY GIVING A CURSE TO FEEL
THE PRESENCE OF EMPTINESS.

21

LOVE TO BE YOURS

<u>LOVE TO BE YOURS</u>

LOVE TO BE YOURS .
THERE WAS A LOT OF REASON WHY
I WAITED TO LEAVE EVERYTHING BEHIND
BUT THERE WAS A SINGLE REASON YOU?
YES YOU .
WHO PULLED ME BACK AND SAID WE
WILL BE TOGETHER AND PASS THE STORM .
THE VOICE OF YOURS UPLIFTING
THE EXHAUSTED SOUL.
MY EYES WERE DIENG TO SEE YOU ONCE .
MY WHOLE PRESSURE FEELS WORTHLESS
WITHOUT YOUR EXISTENCE .
THE WAY YOU SMILE MAKE ME FEEL ALIVE .
I UNDERSTOOD THE REASON WHY I AM ALIVE .
I UNDERTOOD THE PLAY OF DESTINY
TO HOLD US TOGETHER.

Printed by Libri Plureos GmbH in Hamburg,
Germany